The Sleepover Club

Have you been invited to all these Sleepovers?

First published in Great Britain by Collins in 1997
Collins is an imprint of HarperCollins *Publishers* Ltd
77-85 Fulham Palace Road, Hammersmith,
London, W6 8JB

3 5 7 9 8 6 4 2

ISBN 0 00 675334 5

Printed and bound in Great Britain by
Caledonian International Book Manufacturing Ltd,
Glasgow G64

Starring the Sleepover Club

by Narinder Dhami

Collins
An imprint of HarperCollins*Publishers*

Please come to a sleepover at
Felicity's

11 Clumber Close
Parklands
Cuddington
Leicester

It's on Friday 11 April.
Please come at 6.30pm
and sleepover till
Saturday morning.

Don't forget, we'll be making
our Sleepover Club video – come
prepared to be a star!

Sleepover Kit List

1. Sleeping bag
2. Pillow
3. Pyjamas (nice ones, for the video)
4. Slippers
5. Toothbrush, toothpaste, soap etc
6. Towel
7. Teddy
8. A creepy story
9. Yummy food for a midnight feast
10. Torch
11. Hairbrush
12. Hair things, like a bobble or hairband, if you need them
13. Clean knickers and socks
14. Sleepover diary and membership card
15. Best clothes for looking cool on video!

CHAPTER ONE

Oh, hi! It's you again. Look, you can walk with me if you want to. I'm going to the video shop to borrow a film. But you've got to promise me one thing. You've got to promise that you won't ask me what happened at our sleepover last night. I can't tell you because it's a Big Secret. The Biggest. So don't ask me, OK?

My mum and dad said I could choose a film for the three of us to watch tonight. Usually one of them comes to the video shop with me and makes a big song and dance about which films are suitable, and which films aren't. You know what parents are like.

But today they said I could come on my own. I think it's because they're pretty relieved that nothing happened at the sleepover last night (or so they think). The last time we slept over at Fliss's, we ended up wrecking her mum's kitchen, as well as giving her gruesome neighbours a complete fit. This time we did something just as bad. We – oh, sorry! I forgot. I can't tell you.

Come on, here's the video shop. No, don't bother going into the adult section. I'm not even allowed to look at the covers of the films over there. Anyway, Nathan Wignall's standing there, trying to pretend he's old enough to borrow a grown-up film. I've told you about Nathan Wignall before, haven't I? He lives next door to me, and he's a complete pain. I could tell you loads of embarrassing stuff about Nathan Wignall, but I haven't got time right now.

We sometimes watch a video when we have a sleepover, but not every time. Like last night at Fliss's, we – whoops, there I go again! Me and my big mouth.

No, I can't tell you. Don't ask me to. My lips are sealed.

Look, don't get mad. Of *course* I trust you. As my grandma always says, if you can't trust your friends, who can you trust? It's just that if our parents find out what really went on at Fliss's house last night, we'll be up to our eyes in everlasting doom for the next five years. So, if I tell you what happened at the sleepover last night, do you swear never to breathe a WORD about it to ANYONE? Cross your heart and hope to die? Do you promise faithfully you won't tell anyone, even if they offer you their last Rolo?

OK, you've twisted my arm. I give in. Let's go behind the children's videos so that no one else can hear us, and I'll tell you all about it.

The sleepover at Fliss's was going to be an ordinary sleepover right up until the day before. Well, what I mean is, no sleepover is ever really ordinary, but we weren't expecting anything special to happen. Of course, we were wrong.

As my grandma always says, the best place to start is at the beginning. That was at school on Thursday morning. We were in the playground, and all of the Sleepover Club were there, except Fliss. Me (I'm Frankie, remember?), Kenny, Rosie and Lyndz. We were discussing our new teacher, Miss Jenkins. Our real teacher, Mrs Weaver, was ill and she hadn't been at school all week. We missed her a bit. But not a lot. Compared to Mrs Weaver, Miss Jenkins was a pushover.

"OK, today I'm going for it," Kenny said. "I bet I can make six trips to the pencil sharpener before Miss Jenkins tells me off."

"What's the record so far?" I asked.

"I managed five times yesterday," said Rosie.

Kenny shrugged. "You only got the fifth one because Danny McCloud had stuffed two rubbers up his nose. You sneaked over to the sharpener while Miss Jenkins was telling him off."

"Then they got stuck up there," said Lyndz. "Poor old Miss Jenkins had a terrible time trying to pull them out."

"I'm glad I'm not a teacher," I said with feeling. "I wouldn't put my fingers up Danny McCloud's nose for a billion pounds."

"Well, she couldn't just let Danny

suffocate, could she?" said Lyndz.

There was a thoughtful silence.

"I wouldn't have a problem with that," Kenny said with a perfectly straight face, and Rosie and I began to giggle.

"I think you're horrible," said Lyndz. "Poor Miss Jenkins. I feel—"

"Really sorry for her!" we all chimed in. Lyndz has got a heart of pure marshmallow.

"Oh, shut up!" Lyndz grinned, and stuck her tongue out at us. She's used to us winding her up. "By the way, where's Fliss?"

"Yeah, where *is* Fliss?" said Kenny. "She's going to be late if she doesn't get here soon."

We all looked at each other. Fliss is never late for school. She's the sort of person who's never late for anything, not even the dentist.

"Look, there she is." Rosie pointed across the playground. "What's the matter with her?"

Fliss was racing madly across the playground towards us, waving her arms in the air. Her face was bright red, and she was puffing and panting like she'd just run the London Marathon. She was so out of breath that, when she skidded to a halt in front of us, she couldn't speak.

"What is it, Fliss?" I asked, feeling a bit alarmed.

Fliss took a huge breath.

"My mum and Andy have bought a camcorder, and my mum says we can video the sleepover tomorrow night!" she squealed.

"Really?" Rosie gasped, her eyes as round as dinner plates.

"Coo-el!" shrieked Kenny and Lyndz.

"You lucky thing, Fliss!" I said. I was green with jealousy. I'd been nagging my mum and dad for months to buy a camcorder. I'd tried everything from bribery (promising to do the dishes for a year), to tugging at the parental heartstrings (asking them how they'd feel when they had no videos of their little girl to watch when I'd grown up). My dad had said, "Relieved". I think he was joking.

"This is so cool," Kenny said happily. "We're going to have an official Sleepover Club video!"

"I'm going to ask my mum if I can get some

new pyjamas," Lyndz babbled excitedly.

"Me too," I said. My favourite Snoopy pyjamas were a bit too old and uninteresting to be on a video. Come to think of it, my sleeping bag was a bit old and uninteresting as well. I could do with a new one. That meant I was going to have to do some major sweet-talking to my mum and dad when I got home tonight.

Fliss was looking as smug as a cat who's eaten twenty cartons of cream. "That's not all," she said. "Andy says he'll make some copies of the video so that everyone can have their own."

That knocked us all out. We couldn't believe it.

"Fliss, you're the best," Kenny said enthusiastically.

Fliss beamed.

"We'll be able to watch our videos and remember what it was like to be in the Sleepover Club, when we're all old and wrinkly," she said.

"We can still carry on having sleepovers when we get old, though, can't we?" Lyndz asked anxiously.

"Course we can," I said. "But just in case we get too old and creaky to play International Gladiators—"

"Or in case we get too old and tired to stay up for midnight feasts," said Kenny.

"Or if we haven't got any teeth left to eat the midnight feasts," Rosie said.

"—we'll always have the videos to remind us," Fliss finished off.

"Oh, I can't wait for tomorrow night," Lyndz sighed. "It's going to be excellent."

We didn't know it then, but we wouldn't need a video to remind us of that sleepover at Fliss's. It was going to be a long, long time before any of us forgot it.

CHAPTER TWO

As I said before, I was really set on having new pyjamas for the Sleepover Event of the Century, so I started my campaign as soon as I got home that night.

"Mum," I said casually, "have you seen my Snoopy pyjamas recently?"

"Is that a trick question?" My mum was putting a family-size packet of vegetarian lasagne in the microwave. No-one cooks in our house, except for my dad's famous pizzas. We're a strictly "heat 'n' eat" family. "I saw them yesterday when I took them out of the washing-machine."

"No, I mean have you seen the state of

them." I pulled my Snoopy pyjamas from behind my back like a magician producing a white rabbit, and flapped them at my mum. "Look at them, they're gross."

My mum raised her eyebrows.

"I can't see anything wrong with them."

"Look!" I showed her the pyjama bottoms. One of the legs had started fraying after a sleepover at Rosie's when Kenny had grabbed me by the ankles and tried to throw me off the bed. I'd kind of helped it along a bit with my nail scissors. "I can't wear these at Fliss's sleepover tomorrow."

"Oh, Frankie, they're perfectly all right."

"No, they aren't," I persisted. Nagging is the only way to wear parents down. They'll do anything for a bit of peace and quiet. "I told you before, Fliss's mum is going to video the sleepover, and I need to look good."

"Frankie," my mum said, "this is a home video, not a Hollywood movie."

"I know. But these pyjamas are dangerous. What if they keep on unravelling while I'm asleep, and they unravel right up to my neck and strangle me?"

My mum looked at me over the top of her glasses.

"Have you been reading those 'Bonechillers' again?"

"Mum," I said solemnly, "I'm being straight with you here. I cannot wear these pyjamas to Fliss's sleepover tomorrow night."

"Fine." My mum opened the fridge and took out a packet of ready-washed salad. "It's lucky you have at least eight other pairs of pyjamas in your cupboard to choose from, then, isn't it?"

"Oh, Mum," I groaned. "Those aren't sleepover pyjamas. And anyway, they're all too small for me."

My mum shrugged. "That's life, Frankie."

Parents. They're so unreasonable. But I wasn't finished yet. I went out of the kitchen, and into the living-room where my dad was laying the table and watching the news on the telly at the same time.

"Guess what, Dad?" I gave him my Best-Behaved Daughter of the Year smile. "Fliss's mum's bought a camcorder, and she's going to video our sleepover tomorrow."

"Really," my dad said absently, his eyes

fixed on the TV.

"So I was hoping I could get a new pair of pyjamas. Could you pick me up after school tomorrow and drive me into Leicester?"

"Sure, sweetheart."

Like taking sweets from a baby.

"Thanks, Dad!" I said, just as my mum came in with the plates.

"Thanks for what?" she asked suspiciously.

"Er – yes, thanks for what?" The news had finished now, and my dad was looking bewildered.

"Dad says he'll drive me into town after school tomorrow to buy some new pyjamas for the sleepover," I said.

My mum put the plates down on the table with a thump.

"Francesca Theresa Thomas, you are the most cunning and devious child I've ever met."

"That's what comes of having lawyers for parents," I said. "By the way, my sleeping bag's looking a bit gross too."

"Don't push your luck, Frankie," said my dad.

"OK, OK. But I really do need new jim-jams.

I want to look good in our video."

"So," said my dad, "we're finally going to see what goes on at these famous sleepovers, are we?"

"I already know what goes on," my mum said, dishing up the lasagne. "Chaos, trouble and lots of junk food."

"There's a bit more to it than that," I said, picking up my fork. "And anyway, we aren't going to let just anyone watch the video. Sleepovers are supposed to be a secret."

Especially from parents. I wasn't quite sure how we were going to get away with keeping what we did at our sleepovers a secret if Fliss's mum was going to be filming us. But I'd worry about that later.

First of all, though, we had to get through Friday at school. It was pretty difficult because we were all hyper-excited about the sleepover that night, and by the end of the day, we'd turned Miss Jenkins into a nervous wreck. Kenny had managed a record eleven trips to the pencil sharpener without being spotted, and we'd played Pass the Sniff in silent reading until our noses hurt.

As soon as the home bell rang, the Sleepover Club were first out of the classroom door.

"My dad's taking me shopping," I told the others. "I'm going to get some new pyjamas for tonight."

"I've already got some," said Kenny. "They're so cool. They're going to be the coolest pyjamas ever seen on video.'"

"What are they like?" asked Lyndz, but Kenny shook her head.

"You'll have to wait and see!"

"Oh, I can't wait for tonight!" Fliss squealed, and we all grinned. Tonight was going to be really special.

I got a wicked pair of pyjamas in Leicester. They were bright orange – I mean really bright, the colour of an ice lolly – and they had apples and bananas printed all over them. There was a matching pair of fluffy orange slippers too, although I had to promise to wash up the dinner plates for two weeks to get my hands on those. By the time we got back home, I had an hour to get ready for the sleepover.

First I packed my sleepover kit. In went my

new pyjamas and slippers, my diary, my toothbrush, my teddy bear, Stanley, a big bag of fun-size Mars bars, a family-size pack of cheese and onion crisps, my torch and personal stuff like a hairbrush and deodorant. Next I had to decide what I was going to wear. Usually we just wear jeans and tee-shirts, so that we can slob out and do exactly what we like, but tonight was different. Tonight I was going to wear my black hipster flares and my new lime-green shirt. And I was going to crimp my hair.

I don't crimp my hair very often, because it takes ages, but I really wanted to look good in our sleepover video. After I'd done my hair, I painted my nails silver. I love silver nail varnish, and I'm allowed to wear it sometimes at weekends, if The Oldies are in a good mood. I was hoping that tonight I could get away without them noticing.

Wait a minute, the man at the video shop desk is giving us funny looks. Maybe we ought to pretend we're looking at the films. Come on, Nathan's over the other side of the shop now, so we should be OK. Just keep an eye out for him, that's all.

Well, when I finally made it downstairs, carrying my sleepover kit and my sleeping bag, my dad raised his eyebrows.

"What happened to that scruffy little girl who used to be our daughter?" he said to my mum.

"Oh, zip it, Dad," I said. "I just threw on the first things I could find."

"It looks like you just threw on some silver nail varnish too," said my mum.

"This is a special occasion, Mum," I said. "When I'm a famous actress, people will be paying thousands of pounds to get their hands on this video."

Did I mention to you that I want to be an actress when I grow up? That's why I was really looking forward to tonight. It was going to be my very first chance to see myself on film.

"Come on then, Michelle Pfeiffer," said my mum, "I'll run you over to Fliss's."

"OK," I said. Fliss doesn't live that far away from us, but I had all my sleepover stuff to carry, and besides, it looked like it was going to rain, which would wash all the crimping out of my hair quicker than you can say "Bad Hair Day".

"Mum," I said when we were in the car and on our way, "can we—?"

"No," said my mum.

"What do you mean, no?" I glared at her. "You didn't even know what I was going to say."

"Oh, yes I do." My mum turned into Fliss's road. "You were going to say, 'Can we get a camcorder?'"

I was speechless. Parents can really make you mad sometimes, can't they?

"Well, why can't we?"

"Because they're too expensive, that's why," my mum said. "Do you know how much they cost, Frankie? Six or seven hundred pounds. Which reminds me." We stopped at some traffic lights, and she turned to look hard at me. "No fooling around tonight. Do exactly what Fliss's mum tells you. Because if anything happens to that camcorder, you and your friends are going to be paying for it out of your pocket money for a very, very long time."

"Oh, Mum," I groaned as we pulled up outside Fliss's house. "Have I ever let you down before?"

"Yes, you have."

"Bye, then," I said quickly, and dived out of the car before she could get launched on a list of sleepover disasters.

I was just about to open Fliss's gate when Kenny's dad's car pulled up, and Kenny jumped out. I stared at her. She was still wearing her Leicester City top because that's all she ever wore when she wasn't at school. But she wasn't wearing her favourite pair of jeans with holes in the knees or her Timberland boots. Instead she was wearing brand-new jeans and proper shoes. With heels. And she'd only gone and crimped her hair.

"You've crimped your hair!" I said.

"So have you!" Kenny stared back at me, and we both started to laugh. "We're going to look like twins on this video!"

A little red car stopped by the kerb while we were still laughing. Rosie's mum waved to us from the driver's seat, and then Rosie got out. She looked really cool in a long skirt and a matching top. And her hair was crimped.

Rosie looked at me and Kenny, and her face went pink.

"You've crimped your hair!" she gasped.

"I think we've already had this conversation," said Kenny.

"We're triplets now!" I said, and we all started to giggle.

Then I looked over Kenny's shoulder, and saw Lyndz walking up the road with her brother Tom. Lyndz looked good in a pink skirt and a black top. But guess what she'd done to her hair?

"Oh-oh," I said. "Crimped hair alert!"

"Oh!" Lyndz gasped when she saw the rest of us. "You've—"

"Crimped your hair!" we all chimed in. "Just like you!"

"Wow," Tom said, grinning all over his face. "Looks like a hairdresser's worst nightmare."

Lyndz gave him a shove.

"Get lost, moron," she said.

Still laughing, Tom went off, and we all stood outside Fliss's house, and looked at each other and our crimped hair.

"Oh, well," said Lyndz with a big grin, "I think we all look great."

"Come on," Kenny said, pushing open the gate. "I'm dying to get inside and get filmed!"

We all hurried up the path. I rang the bell, and Fliss opened the door. She was wearing a spotless, cream-coloured lacy dress with matching tights and shoes, and her hair was piled high on her head. It had been stuck with pins all over to keep it up, and it looked pretty uncomfortable. She took one look at our hair, and burst out laughing.

"You've all crimped your hair!"

"Yes, we had noticed," I said.

"Is that the girls, Fliss?" Andy, Fliss's mum's boyfriend, came out of the living-room with a camcorder balanced on his shoulder. He stopped and moved it slowly in our direction. Immediately we all started squealing and giggling and shoving each other.

"Come on, girls, give us a smile!" Andy said.

We all began to wave and smile at the camera. This was certainly going to be one sleepover we would never forget.

CHAPTER THREE

So there we all were, sitting in a row on Mrs Sidebotham's cream-coloured sofa, trying not to look bored out of our skulls. Which we were, actually.

"Oh, come on, girls." Andy sighed from behind the camcorder. "Do something interesting, can't you?"

We all looked down at our feet. Andy sighed again, and lowered the camcorder.

"What's the matter with you?" he said, "You don't usually sit here and do nothing when you come round for one of these sleepovers, do you?"

We all looked at each other. No, of course

we didn't usually sit there and do nothing when we had a sleepover. But today was different. Today we were being filmed, and although Andy wasn't exactly Fliss's real dad, he was still sort of like a parent. That meant that some of the things we might have done, we couldn't do. So the safest thing was to sit on the sofa and do absolutely nothing. After all, as my grandma says, why go looking for trouble?

When we'd first arrived at Fliss's, it had been fun being filmed. Fliss's mum had made a great big tea, and we'd all sat down to eat, while Andy kept dodging around the table trying to film us all. It took us about ten minutes to get over the urge to wave and grin like an idiot every time he pointed the camera in our direction, and then after that we were OK.

It was after tea was over that things started to go wrong. If it had been a normal sleepover, there were lots of things we could have done. Sometimes we just used to sit and talk, until it was time to go to bed. But a lot of the things we talked about were Private and Top Secret, and we didn't feel like talking about things like that with Andy and his camcorder sticking to us like glue.

One of the other things we do when we go to Fliss's is think of ways to annoy her snobby neighbours. They're called Charles and Jessica Watson-Wade (yes, really) and they have a baby called Bruno, which I thought was a dog's name. The last time we slept over at Fliss's, we had a killer of a time winding-up the Watson-Wades. Fliss's mum went mad (and so did every other mum and dad), but it was worth it. The problem was, how could we play Winding-up the Watson-Wades when Andy and his camera were right behind us?

So Kenny had suggested that we played barging contests, one of our International Gladiators games. One person's the horse, the other's the rider, and you have to barge the other horse and rider off the lawn in the back garden. We always play barging contests when we sleepover at Fliss's, because there's not much else we can do. Fliss's bedroom is too small for really tough stuff, and we can't do anything inside because her mum is so house-proud. But the garden's quite big, and we can play barging contests out there as much as we want to.

Not today, though. Fliss had gone pale at the very thought.

"I can't, not with my hair up like this," she'd said. "It'd drop down in one minute flat."

"I don't want to play either," Lyndz said. "I've got to keep my new clothes clean."

Rosie didn't say anything, but she didn't look too keen herself. That was probably because she was wearing a long skirt, and she'd have to hitch it up and tuck it into her knickers. I didn't say anything either. I didn't want to get my best ankle boots dirty. After all, it had taken me three months to persuade my parents to buy them.

Kenny had rolled her eyes, looking disgusted.

"What a bunch of wimps," she said, but we wouldn't give in. No barging contests. And that was why we were all sitting in a row of the sofa, bored out of our minds and twiddling our thumbs, which is definitely not what a sleepover is supposed to be about.

"Are you all having a good time, girls?"

Fliss's mum asked us brightly as she came into the living-room.

"Yes, thank you, Mrs Sidebotham," we all said dutifully, lying through our teeth.

"If you hear me snoring, pinch me," Kenny whispered in my ear. I bit my lip to stop myself from laughing, but Andy was still onto us like a shot.

"What did you say to Frankie, Kenny?" he asked eagerly. "Come on, say it again and I can video it."

Kenny shook her head.

"I can't," she said solemnly. "It was secret sleepover business."

"Oh." Andy looked really disappointed. "Well, you girls must want to do *something*?"

There was a note of desperation in his voice, which made me feel quite sorry for him.

"Why don't you play Monopoly?" suggested Fliss's mum.

"Oh, great big fat hairy deal," I heard Kenny mutter. It's not that we don't like Monopoly, we do. It was just that we thought our sleepover video would be a bit more radical than this.

Fliss went off to get the Monopoly box, but by this time Andy had had enough, and said he was off to the pub. So Fliss's mum took over the camera. She didn't film the whole game, which was lucky because it went on for hours. She filmed the beginning, then she stopped to watch *Brookside*, and then she filmed the end, when Rosie won. Rosie had Mayfair and Park Lane, and she cleaned the rest of us out.

"Right, time for you girls to go up to bed," Fliss's mum said when we'd finished the game. "I thought it might be nice if I filmed you going up the stairs, and waving goodnight. Then you can watch the video in the morning before you go home."

By this time I was sick of being filmed, and I think the others were too, but we couldn't very well say so, could we? So we trailed out into the hall, and followed each other up the stairs. Fliss's mum stood at the bottom, shouting instructions at us.

"Come on, girls, turn around and wave at me. Nice big smiles. No, Kenny, we don't want to see your tongue, thank you."

"Aren't you coming upstairs with us, Mrs

Sidebotham?" asked Lyndz. "You could film us putting on our new pyjamas."

Fliss's mum looked shocked. "Oh no, Lyndsey. I don't think that would be very nice at all."

"But you don't get to see anything," said Kenny. "We change inside our sleeping bags. It's a great laugh."

Fliss's mum shook her head firmly. "No, I don't think so. Now off you go. It's getting late."

We all trailed upstairs, and into Fliss's bedroom. I honestly couldn't remember a more boring sleepover. And to think we'd all been so excited… Even Fliss looked miserable.

No one said anything in front of Fliss, but when she'd gone to the bathroom, Kenny flopped onto one of the beds, and groaned.

"I hope no-one ever watches that video, or they'll think that sleepovers are some kind of punishment," she said.

"Tonight was the pits," I said. "I've had more fun at the dentist's."

"Don't say anything to Fliss," Lyndz said. "It wasn't her fault. We all wanted to be filmed too."

We all nodded, and trailed gloomily over to our bags to get our pyjamas. Sleepovers were supposed to be fun, and this one definitely wasn't. For just about the first time ever at a sleepover, I wished I was back at home in my bedroom, on my own. Oh well, I told myself, the best part of the sleepover hadn't happened yet.

I cheered up a bit when I opened my bag, and saw my brand-new orange pyjamas.

"Wow, they're really wild," said Lyndz, who was looking over my shoulder. "Look at mine." Lyndz's new jim-jams were yellow with big pink flowers all over them.

"They're not as cool as mine," said Kenny. She took her pyjamas out of her bag, and we all burst out laughing. They were black, with white skulls all over them.

"They're a killer, aren't they?" said Kenny. "I got them from a boy's shop. I had to nag my mum like crazy to get them. She said they'd give me nightmares."

Rosie grabbed her bag, and pulled out her own pyjamas, which had teddy-bears all over them.

"Bet you I'm changed first!" she yelled, diving into her sleeping bag. We all squealed, and leapt into our own sleeping-bags, pulling off our clothes as fast as we could. I joined in, although I always lose. I'm just too tall and my arms and legs are too long. I didn't mind not winning though, because it was a good laugh. And, boy, it was the first good laugh we'd had all evening.

Fliss came back from the bathroom just as we all finished changing. She still looked a bit miserable.

"Oh, come on, Fliss, cheer up," said Rosie. "I've brought toffee popcorn for the midnight feast, and you can have it all if you want."

Fliss loves toffee popcorn. Her face lit up.

"Thanks, Rosie," she said, but she didn't have time to say anything else because just then Lyndz hit Kenny right on the behind with a squishy-poo (that's a sleeping bag filled with clothes, in case you didn't know). Kenny went flying, and landed on one of the beds with her bottom in the air. We all screamed with laughter, and started belting each other with our own squishy-poos. This sleepover was getting better by the minute.

By the time Fliss's mum put her head round the door twenty minutes later, we were all tucked up. Fliss and Rosie were in the two beds, and Kenny, Lyndz and I were in our sleeping bags between them on the floor.

"Goodnight, girls," she said. "Sleep tight."

"Goodnight."

She closed the door. We lay there in the dark and counted up to twenty-five, then we switched our torches on.

"What shall we do first?" Fliss asked.

"Eat!" the rest of us said.

I don't know why we bother calling them midnight feasts, because we never make it to midnight. We always seem to be starving the moment we switch our torches on.

"This is the best bit of sleepovers," said Lyndz, handing round some chocolate biscuits.

"Yeah, this is the real sleepover, what's happening now. It's a pity we can't film it," said Kenny.

And of course, that's where the disaster really started...

CHAPTER FOUR

So there we were having our midnight feast, and Kenny had just said that it was a shame we couldn't film the stuff we did after lights out. Everybody agreed with her, but nobody really thought much about it at the time. Instead, we ate all the crisps and chocolates we'd brought (and Fliss ate most of Rosie's popcorn), and then we wrote in our diaries.

"What shall we do now?" Lyndz asked, when we'd finished writing.

"We could tell jokes," I suggested.

"No, let's have stories," said Kenny. "Horror stories."

"No," Fliss wailed. "They give me nightmares."

"I think we should do what Fliss wants," said Rosie. "After all, it's her sleepover."

"I want to practise our dance routine for next Friday," Fliss said firmly.

We're always working out dance routines. It's one of our best skives because we get to practise them in the school hall when all the other kids have been chucked out to play in the cold. Mrs Poole, our headteacher, lets us do the routines in Friday assembly, which is always a great laugh.

"Good idea," said Lyndz.

So we all got out of our beds and sleeping bags, and lined up in the space between the two beds. Fliss's bedroom isn't very big, so we had to stand on top of the sleeping bags. When we were all standing next to each other, there wasn't room to move our arms, never mind our legs, but we had a go. Then we got bored with trying to dance in such a tiny space, and instead we started pushing each other off the floor and onto the beds. Once you were bounced onto a bed, you were out. Eventually there was just me and Rosie left, and I really had to give her a mighty shove to get her off the floor. She bounced onto Fliss's bed, and landed right on top of Kenny.

"Oi!" Kenny spluttered. "Do you mind!" She picked up the nearest pillow, and hit out at her. Rosie ducked smartly, and the pillow thwacked Lyndz round the head instead. It was like something out of a silent movie.

By this time we were all laughing so hard, my sides really hurt.

"Sssh!" Fliss pleaded between giggles. "You'll wake my mum up!"

"Oh, that was excellent," I said, flopping down on the bed next to Kenny. "I wish I had a picture of Lyndz's face when Kenny hit her with that pillow!"

"We would have had a picture of it if we were filming with the camcorder," said Kenny.

"OK, OK," said Fliss impatiently. "But I don't know what you expect me to do about it."

I could see Kenny's eyes glinting wickedly in the light of my torch.

"Well, we could film ourselves..."

Fliss turned so white, she looked like a

ghost. So did Rosie. Even I was a bit taken aback, and I'm used to Kenny's mad ideas.

"What?" said Lyndz, who's sometimes a bit slow on the uptake. "How could we do that?"

"Simple," said Kenny. "Fliss borrows the camcorder, and then we can film ourselves doing real Sleepover Club things."

"NO," said Fliss.

"OK, OK, don't get in a razz," said Kenny. "If you don't know how to work the camcorder, just say so."

"It's not that," said Fliss quickly. She hates us to think that she can't do anything and everything. "Andy showed me how to use it when he wanted me to film him and mum doing the garden."

Kenny shrugged.

"So what's the problem then?"

Fliss opened her mouth, then closed it again. I guessed that what she'd been about to say was that she wasn't allowed to touch the camcorder unless her mum or Andy were around to supervise.

"Camcorders are really expensive," said Rosie. "I don't think Fliss's mum would be too pleased if we used it without her permission."

Fliss shrugged. "I can do it, no problem," she said airily. "I'll fetch it now."

"Nice one, Fliss!" Kenny began applauding, and so did Lyndz. I was pleased too. After all, the official sleepover video had been about as interesting as watching paint dry so far. But I couldn't help hearing my mum's voice faintly in the back of my mind. "Remember if anything happens to that camcorder, you and your friends will be paying for it out of your pocket-money for years to come..."

I pushed the thought away.

"Come with me, Frankie," Fliss was saying nervously. "I don't want to go on my own."

"Where are we going?" I asked.

"To the spare bedroom. That's where my mum keeps the camcorder." Fliss picked up her torch, and gave the others a warning look. "The rest of you be quiet until we get back."

Fliss and I went out onto the dark landing. Fliss's mum and Andy were in bed, and so was her brother Callum. I have to say, it gave me a really funny feeling to be creeping about someone else's house in the dark in the middle of the night. I felt like a burglar.

"This is the spare room." Fliss stopped so suddenly that I bumped right into her. "We've got to be careful. The door squeaks like mad."

I reached for the handle and pushed the door open a little way. It gave a loud, frightening creak, the kind of noise you'd expect if you were entering a haunted house. My heart began to bump, and my hands felt clammy.

"Sssh!" Fliss whispered.

"I couldn't help it," I hissed back. I gave the door one more tiny shove, so that it was just open wide enough for us to squeeze in. It gave another ear-splitting creak, and we held our breath. But no-one came to see what was going on.

We slipped inside.

"Hold the torch while I get the camcorder out of the cupboard," Fliss said in my ear.

Curiously I played the torch around the room while Fliss was getting the camcorder. I'd never been in the spare bedroom before, and it didn't look anything like our spare bedroom at home. Our spare room is full of junk and bits and pieces like headless Sindy dolls, old newspapers and cookery books no-one uses. But Fliss's spare room was done up like a house in a magazine. There were flouncy blinds at the windows which matched the cover on the bed, and there were cupboards built all along one wall. There was also a headless person standing in the corner.

I couldn't help gasping, even though I clapped my hand over my mouth to muffle the sound. Fliss jumped a mile into the air, and nearly dropped the camcorder box.

"What's the matter with you?" she said under her breath.

"Did you know there's a headless person over there in the corner?" I said breathlessly.

"That's my mum's dress-making dummy, you idiot." Fliss pushed me towards the door. "Come on. If anyone wakes up, we're dead."

We hurried back to Fliss's bedroom. As soon as we got there, the others crowded round us as Fliss put the camcorder box carefully on the bed.

"Excellent!" said Kenny. "Come on, let's get started."

"Just a minute," said Lyndz. "Fliss's mum is going to know we borrowed the camcorder, isn't she?"

"What do you mean?" asked Kenny.

"Well, when we watch the video tomorrow morning, she's going to see all the bits we record now, when we're supposed to be asleep," said Lyndz.

We all looked at each other.

"Oh, rats," said Kenny. "What do we do now?"

"Easy," said Rosie. "We take the film out of the camcorder when we've finished, and put in a new blank tape. Then Andy and Fliss's mum will think it didn't record for some reason."

We all stared admiringly at Rosie. My mum says I'm devious, but I'm just a beginner compared to Rosie.

"Excellent idea," said Kenny. "Fliss, you have got a spare blank tape, haven't you?"

Fliss nodded.

"We've got loads."

"Great." Kenny gave a sigh of relief, and opened the camcorder box. "OK, let's get started!"

"We'll have to put the light on," I said. "Our torches won't be bright enough."

"What if someone sees the light under my door?" Fliss said nervously.

"Oh, you just put some clothes or a towel down to block it out," said Rosie. "I do it all the time when I want to read late. My mum never knows."

It was right at that very moment that we heard footsteps coming softly down the hall.

"Quick!" hissed Lyndz. "Someone's coming!"

For a second we were all frozen to the spot. Then we turned off our torches, and leapt for our beds and sleeping bags. Because Fliss's room is so small and we were so panicked, we kept bumping into each other in the dark before we managed to grope our way to our beds. It took me a few seconds to fold all my arms and legs in, and it was only when I was safely inside with my eyes tight shut that I remembered the box with the camcorder in it. But it was too late now.

Someone was opening the door...

CHAPTER FIVE

It was Fliss's mum. She put her head round the door and whispered, "Are you girls asleep?"

No one made a sound. I don't know about the others, but I was holding my breath so hard my lungs were bursting. Fliss's mum stood there looking into the room for what seemed like hours. Then she shut the door gently, and we could hear her footsteps going down the landing. We waited until we heard her bedroom door close. Then we all sat up, and Kenny crept across the room and flipped the light switch on.

"Wow, that was close," she said. "We only

just made it."

"I thought she'd see the camcorder on Rosie's bed, and we'd be done for," said Lyndz. "She must have heard Fliss and Frankie walking around."

Fliss was as white as a sheet.

"Thank goodness my mum didn't notice the camcorder!"

"By the way, where *is* the camcorder?" I said.

We all looked at Rosie's bed. We'd left the camcorder box sitting right there on the pink bedcover. But it wasn't there now.

"Don't panic," said Rosie calmly. She threw back her duvet cover, and there was the box nestling underneath. "I managed to grab it just before Mrs Sidebotham came in."

Fliss almost collapsed with relief.

"Thanks, Rosie," was all she could manage to say.

"Come on, then, are we going to make a video or what?" Impatiently Kenny grabbed the box, and began pulling the cardboard flaps open.

"Be careful!" Fliss hissed under her breath. "Let me do it!"

We all waited expectantly as Fliss unwrapped the camcorder from its box as carefully as if it was the Crown Jewels.

"We ought to decide what we're going to do," said Lyndz.

"Oh, don't be so boring," said Kenny. "Let's just mess around. What do you reckon, Rosie?"

"Yeah, that sounds cool," Rosie agreed. "As long as Fliss doesn't mind," she added quickly.

Fliss was too busy fiddling with the camcorder to hear.

"Right, I'm going to start recording," she announced, putting the machine up to her eye. "I'm starting now."

Kenny immediately leapt forward and stuck her face right up to the lens.

"Welcome to the Sleepover Club!" she said with a huge grin.

Fliss leapt backwards as if she'd been bitten.

"You nearly frightened me to death, Kenny!" she said, while the rest of us rolled around in fits of laughter. "Do it properly, or I'll put the camcorder away right now."

"OK, Mum," said Kenny. "How about this then?"

She grabbed a hairbrush from Fliss's dressing-table, and spoke into it as if it was a microphone.

"We'd like to welcome you all to this very special meeting of the Sleepover Club. My name is Kenny, and if you ever call me Laura MacKenzie, I'll thump you."

"Don't make me laugh," Fliss said between giggles, "or the camera will shake too much."

"Let me introduce you to the other members," Kenny said into her hairbrush. "This is Lyndsey Collins, known as Lyndz." Kenny pointed at Lyndz, who was sitting on Fliss's bed. "She's the nicest person I know, and she's always got the hiccups."

"Oh, don't, Kenny!" Lyndz said in between giggles, as Fliss turned the camera on her. "Don't start me off!"

"Well, you ought to be hiccuping," said Kenny. "It won't be a proper sleepover if you don't. Come on, can't you manage just one little hiccup for the camera?"

Just for once, Lyndz couldn't. She was

laughing so hard she had to hide her head under Fliss's pillow.

"Over here, Fliss." Kenny pointed at me. "Frankie next. Come on, Fliss, do I have to be the director as well as the star?"

"Give me a chance," Fliss moaned, turning the camera slowly in my direction.

"This is Frankie, my best mate," said Kenny. "No, you're not seeing things. She really is as tall as a house. We reckon her parents water her with liquid manure every night."

"Shut up, lamebrain," I said, and chucked a pillow at her.

"And this is Rosie..." Kenny waited for Fliss to turn slowly in her direction. "Rosie's got loads of good ideas for fooling parents. She's really cool." Kenny chucked the hairbrush onto the bed, "OK, that's everyone."

"What about me?" Fliss wailed from behind the camera.

"Oh, yeah, sorry, I forgot about you. Here," Kenny held out her hand, "give me the camera and I can film you. Then we'll all be in it."

"No way," said Fliss. "No one's doing any videotaping except me."

Kenny shrugged. "Please yourself." She picked up her hairbrush again. "Sorry, I missed out Fliss. Fliss is the Queen of the Sleepover Club, because this is her sleepover and her camcorder, and she's letting us use it, which is really excellent."

Fliss grinned.

"That's better," she said. "Now stop hogging the camera, Kenny. Let someone else have a go."

"It's a shame we've eaten our midnight feast," said Lyndz. "We could have filmed ourselves stuffing our faces."

"Never mind, you can talk about it instead," said Kenny, and she pushed the hairbrush into Lyndz's hand.

Lyndz began to giggle as Fliss turned the camera on her.

"Um – OK, midnight feasts. We always, always have a midnight feast when we sleepover—"

"More like a ten-thirty feast," I butted in.

"Sssh!" Kenny slung one of Fliss's cuddly toys at me. "Lyndz is talking."

Lyndz wasn't, actually. She was still giggling.

"Stop it, Lyndz!" said Fliss. "Say something interesting."

So Lyndz did. She gave a huge hiccup. We all burst out laughing, and had to bury our heads in our pillows to muffle the sound.

"Don't just – hic! – sit there – hic! – laughing!" said Lyndz. "Someone – hic! – help me!"

We've tried all the usual ways of getting Lyndz's hiccups to stop, but the best way is for someone to press down hard with their thumbs on the palm of her hand while she holds her breath. Don't ask me why this works. It just does.

The others were laughing too hard to be of any use, so I grabbed Lyndz's hand, and pressed down hard. Lyndz held her breath for so long, she started to turn crimson, but when she finally breathed out, her hiccups were gone.

"Thanks, Frankie," she said, gulping in a huge lungful of air.

"Come on," said Fliss impatiently. "I'm wasting loads of tape when you're not doing anything interesting."

"What about our sleepover song?" said Lyndz.

"Yes, let's sing it," said Rosie.

"But we don't sing that till we're about to go to sleep," Kenny groaned.

"We don't have to go to sleep," Lyndz argued. "We can just sing it so Fliss can video us."

"Go on then," said Fliss. "Don't bother with the actions, just do the song."

When we do our sleepover song, we're usually all tucked up in our sleeping bags with our torches on. When we get to the end of the song, the first one of us to lie down flat turns her torch off, and then we carry on till everyone's out.

"You three do the song," said Kenny. "I'm going to have a rest. I'm tired out." She put her hand up to her head and said in a fake American accent, "Being a star is so exhausting."

"Get her," I scoffed. "Come on, let's do the song then."

So we started singing:

"Down by the river there's a hanky-panky

With a bullfrog sitting on the hanky-panky—"

I could just see Kenny looking in her sleepover bag out of the corner of my eye.

"—With an Ooh Aah, Ooh Aah,

Hey, Mrs Zippy, with a One-Two-Three – OUT!"

Just before we got to "OUT!", which is when we try to be first to lie down if we're doing the actions, Kenny popped up behind us. When we sang "OUT!", she belted Rosie with her teddy bear.

"Ow!" Rosie jumped onto her bed. "I'll get you for that, Kenny!" She grabbed her own teddy bear, and waved it round her head. "Come on then, if you think you're hard enough!"

"Ooh, you don't frighten me!" Kenny scoffed. She jumped onto Rosie's bed, and next minute they were battling away whacking each other with their teddies, trying to knock each other's bear out of their hand. I love teddy fights, because my bear Stanley, who's as tough as old boots, always wins. Stanley was sitting on my pillow looking really left out, so I grabbed him and shoved him under Lyndz's nose.

"Stanley's challenging your bear to a fight to the death," I said.

Lyndz groaned. "Do I have to? We always lose."

"Come on, Lyndz!" I jumped onto Fliss's bed. "You don't want your teddy to be known as the wimp of Teddyland, do you?"

Lyndz grabbed her teddy, and climbed up onto Fliss's bed. We started jumping up and down and whacking each other, while Fliss videoed us.

"Be quiet – please!" Fliss kept pleading from behind the camera, but it's hard to be really quiet when you're playing teddy fights. Anyway, we all know that we can be fairly noisy when we sleep over at Fliss's, because her mum's bedroom is right at the other end of a very long landing. In fact, we know exactly how much noise we can make before Mrs Sidebotham comes charging in to tell us off.

Kenny and Rosie were still fighting it out on the other bed, and Lyndz and I were battling away too. At first I let Lyndz get a few whacks at Stanley in, so she didn't get too downhearted, but then I went in for the kill. Stanley headbutted her bear so hard that Lyndz went flying. She managed to stop herself on the edge of the bed, but she was wobbling so much she couldn't get her balance. She wobbled and she teetered and she wobbled, and for a second or two she looked as if she was going to make it. It was touch and go, and it was so funny that even Kenny and Rosie stopped bashing each other's bears to watch. But in the end the force of gravity was just too much for Lyndz. She went head-over-heels, and landed flat on the floor. Luckily the sleeping bags were piled up in a heap, so she didn't hurt herself, or make too much noise.

"That was brilliant, Lyndz!" I laughed. "Just like a stuntwoman!"

"I loved the way you just wobbled around on the edge of the bed for about five minutes!" said Kenny. "It was so cool."

Lyndz sat up, rubbing her behind.

"Thank goodness the sleeping bags were there, or I might have broken my leg!"

Rosie was looking thoughtful.

"Hey, you know what?" she said, and she sounded really excited. "I've just had a brilliant idea."

And that was when things really started to go downhill...

CHAPTER SIX

Come on, let's choose a film, and I'll tell you the rest of the story on the way home. How about *Mrs Doubtfire*? I've seen it before, but I don't mind seeing it again. I'll just take it up to the counter, and get it checked out.

Right, let's go – and make sure Nathan Wignall isn't following us. I wouldn't put anything past that little creep.

OK, we're in the clear. And remember, you've got to promise not to tell anyone what I'm going to tell you now...

Well, Rosie had this brilliant idea which turned out to be totally non-brilliant, but we all loved it at the time.

"Look," she said, "Why don't we send that video of Lyndz to *You've Been Framed*?"

"What a totally cool idea!" Kenny said immediately. "The Sleepover Club on TV – excellent!"

"We could make loads of money too," Rosie said breathlessly. "They pay for the best videos."

"How much?" Lyndz asked, her eyes wide.

"About two hundred pounds," Rosie said. "Or it might be more."

"Two hundred quid!" Kenny gasped. "I'm in!"

"Before you start counting the money," I said, "there's just one thing you've forgotten. If we end up splashed all over the TV, our parents are going to find out we borrowed the camcorder without Mrs Sidebotham's permission."

We all looked at each other. Then Kenny shrugged. "So what? They'll probably be so proud to see us on TV, they won't care."

"Or we can try to make sure our parents don't see the programme," Rosie chimed in.

"We can talk our way out of it somehow,"

Kenny added. "Come on, Frankie, don't be so boring."

"Oh, all right," I said. I didn't need much persuading. I was dying to be on TV. It was one of my biggest ambitions.

"What about you, Lyndz?" Kenny said. "You're the star, after all."

Lyndz giggled.

"Let's go for it," she agreed, "What do you think, Fliss?"

It was then that we realised that Fliss hadn't said anything for the last five minutes. She was red in the face, and looked completely miserable.

"What's up with you?" I asked her. "You've got a face like a wet week-end."

"We can't send the video to *You've Been Framed*," Fliss muttered.

"Why not?" we all said together.

"I just don't think it's a good idea," Fliss said stiffly.

"Oh, come on, Fliss, don't be a wimp all your life," Kenny urged. "If it does get on TV, we can get round our parents, no problem."

Fliss blushed. "It's not that."

"Well, what then?"

Fliss looked down at her feet. "I wasn't – er – actually filming Lyndz when she fell off the bed," she mumbled. "Sorry."

"What?" We all stared at her.

"You mean you missed the sleepover stunt of the century?" I said. "So what were you doing? Filming Kenny and Rosie on the other bed?"

"Um. No," said Fliss. "I *was* filming the teddy fights. Then I got bored…"

"So what were you filming then?" Rosie asked.

Fliss looked even more sheepish. "My cuddly toys on the windowsill."

"Oh, great big fat hairy deal," said Kenny in disgust. "So now we've got pathetic little cuddly toys in the middle of our radical sleepover vid."

"Plus we've lost the chance to win loads of money," I pointed out.

Lyndz shook her head sadly. "I really wanted to see myself somersaulting off the bed as well," she said.

"I said I was sorry," Fliss muttered miserably.

"Never mind, Fliss," Rosie said quickly.

"I've just thought of something." She turned to Lyndz. "You could do it again, couldn't you, Lyndz?"

"Do what again?" said Lyndz. I told you she was a bit slow on the uptake.

"Wobbling about on the edge of the bed, and somersaulting off it. You could do it again, couldn't you?"

Lyndz looked doubtful.

"I dunno—"

"Course you can!" Rosie grabbed Lyndz's arm, and hauled her onto Fliss's bed. "That's what we've got to do. Lyndz does the stunt again, and this time Fliss videos her!"

"Good idea!" Kenny slapped Rosie on the back. "Don't you think that's a good idea, Fliss?"

Fliss was suddenly looking a lot happier now that she was well and truly off the hook. "Yeah, good one. Come on then, Lyndz."

Lyndz picked up her teddy bear.

"OK, I'll give it a go." Then she frowned. "Isn't it cheating though?"

"No, course not," Kenny said. "I mean, it's not like you didn't do it at all, is it?"

"And anyway," I said, "I swear some of

those videos on the telly are set-ups."

"Well, all right," said Lyndz, and she climbed onto Fliss's bed. "Come on, then, Frankie."

I grabbed Stanley, and Rosie and Kenny sat down on the other bed to watch.

"I can't remember what we did first," said Lyndz. "I think I got in a few whacks at Stanley."

"And then I landed the killer thwack," I said. "That was the one that sent you off the bed. Ready, Fliss?"

"Ready," Fliss called back.

Lyndz and I began whacking each other's teddy bears again, like we'd done the first time. But it wasn't as easy as we thought it would be to do the stunt again. The trouble was, Lyndz was watching me like a hawk, waiting for the big THWACK! So I held off for a bit, then I swung Stanley at her teddy when she wasn't expecting it. Instead of falling spectacularly off the bed, though, Lyndz just sat down – plonk – on the duvet.

"Well, that was hilarious," Kenny said sarcastically.

"This is more difficult than it looks,

smarty-pants," I said.

"I told you I couldn't do it," Lyndz wailed.

"Try again," Fliss said.

Lyndz and I had a few more tries, but it was no good. Lyndz was just too nervous. I managed to knock her off the bed a few times, but there was nothing like the wobbling and somersaulting which had happened the first time. Lyndz was just too scared of hurting herself to try and do that again.

"This is hopeless," I said, after the sixth attempt. "Let's forget it."

"Sorry," Lyndz said, biting her lip.

"Let me and Rosie have a go." Kenny stood up. "I bet we can do it."

"But that's cheating," Lyndz said. "You didn't do it the first time."

"So what?" Kenny shrugged. "We want to get on the TV, don't we?"

"Yeah, but what about me and Lyndz?" I said.

"What about me and Rosie?" Kenny challenged me.

"Well, what about Fliss?" Lyndz chimed in. "She's stuck behind the camera."

We all looked at each other. It was becoming very obvious that, if we were going to send a Sleepover Club video to *You've Been Framed*, we all wanted to be in it.

"So that means we're all going to have to get into the video somehow," said Kenny.

"What, you mean we're all going to have a teddy fight and somersault off the bed at exactly the same time?" I asked sarcastically.

"Ha funny ha," said Kenny. "No, we'll do something else. Something screamingly funny, that we can all be in."

"Except the person who's doing the filming," said Fliss sulkily.

We all rolled our eyes at that.

"Hang on for just one tiny little second, Felicity Sidebotham," I said. "You said nobody was going to do any filming except you."

"I know," Fliss muttered. "But that was before I knew we were going to be on TV."

"Well, someone's got to work the camcorder," said Kenny. "If it's not Fliss, who's going to do it?"

We all looked down at our feet.

"Oh, go on," said Lyndz. "I'll do it. I don't mind."

Fliss looked relieved.

"Thanks, Lyndz. Come over here, and I'll show you how it works. It's dead easy."

"What are we going to do then?" Kenny said to me and Rosie, while Fliss and Lyndz were bent over the camcorder. "It's got to be funny to get on TV."

"They seem to like people falling over," said Rosie.

"And stunts with pets in," I said.

"Right," said Kenny. "Anyone fancy balancing Fliss's goldfish on their nose and then falling down the stairs?"

The three of us giggled.

"Whatever it is, it's got to be good," I said. "*You've Been Framed* must get loads of tapes."

"We could pretend we're sleepwalking," Rosie suggested. "Then we could do all sorts of daft things."

"What, four of us sleepwalking at the same time?" I said doubtfully. "I don't think that'll work."

Kenny's eyes lit up. "Wait a minute, I've got an excellent idea."

"What?" Rosie and I said together.

Kenny winked at us. "You'll have to wait and see. First I've got to try and persuade Fliss to let us go downstairs. There isn't enough room to do it here."

"No chance," Rosie said immediately.

"You obviously haven't seen Kenny sweet-talk anyone before," I muttered in Rosie's ear.

"Fliss, I've got a brilliant idea for our *You've Been Framed* video," Kenny said with a beaming smile.

Fliss raised her eyebrows. "Oh?"

Kenny nodded. "Yep, it's so brilliant, it's sure to get on TV."

Fliss began to look interested. "What is it?"

"Tell you in a minute," said Kenny. "The thing is, there's no room to do it in here. We need to go downstairs."

Fliss looked as though Kenny had asked her to cut her arm off.

"Are you crazy?" she spluttered. "We can't do that! What if my mum hears us?"

"She won't," Kenny said firmly. "Everyone's going to be really quiet."

"No!" Fliss hissed.

"We'll be as quiet as mice—"

"NO!"

"Oh, well, that's a shame." Kenny shrugged her shoulders. "Especially as you would've been the star."

Fliss's eyes widened.

"What?"

"Oh, didn't I say?" Kenny remarked innocently. "You were going to be the star of my idea. Still, never mind."

Fliss frowned. "Well, I suppose we could," she said slowly. "As long as everyone is really quiet..."

"Course we'll be quiet!" Kenny raced eagerly over to the bedroom door. "Come on then, let's go. Lyndz, are you sure you don't mind not being in the video?"

"Course I don't," Lyndz said cheerfully. She picked up the camcorder, and put it up to her eye. "Doing the filming is just as good."

"Come on then," said Kenny. "Let's go downstairs."

"And be quiet," Fliss added nervously.

We all tiptoed over to the door, our hearts thumping. Kenny turned the handle and pulled it open, and we all crept out one by one...

Look, we're not far from my house now, and I've still got the worst bit to tell you. We'd better stop along the way, 'cos I can't tell you what comes next if there's even a sniff of a parent around. Come on, let's sit down on this wall for a while.

CHAPTER SEVEN

Now, where was I? Oh, yeah, I'd just got to the bit where we were all creeping down the stairs, one behind the other. We didn't dare put the light on, so we were shuffling slowly along, trying not to trip over anything. I was in front, and Fliss was behind me, and then the others were behind her. I'm sort of like the Sleepover Club scout – I always get sent on ahead to sniff out the dangers. The others must think I'm dead brave. Or maybe I'm just the only one stupid enough to do it...

"Lyndz?" I heard Fliss whisper behind me. Then, "Ow! Kenny, you dweeb, you walked right into me!"

"Well, don't just stop like that!" I heard Kenny grumbling. "I can't see a thing in the dark."

"I just wanted to ask Lyndz if the camcorder's OK," Fliss whispered.

"What?" That was Lyndz. She was at the end of the line with the camera. "I can't hear you!"

I rolled my eyes. This was getting ridiculous. "Kenny, Fliss wants to ask Lyndz if the camcorder's OK. Pass it on."

Kenny turned round, and whispered.

"Rosie, Fliss wants to know if the camcorder's OK. Pass it on."

We all stood and waited for Rosie to whisper to Lyndz. A few seconds later an answer came back from Kenny.

"The camcorder's fine. It's just got a bit of a headache, that's all."

"Oh, very funny," Fliss said under her breath. The rest of us began to giggle as silently as we could.

"Well, honestly, Fliss," said Kenny. "Keep cool, can't you? It's only a machine, not a person."

"Can we please get a move on?" I hissed.

"If Fliss's mum hears us, we're history."

We carried on shuffling down the stairs, and then we groped our way across the hall and into the living room. I counted in four shadowy figures, and then I closed the door as silently as I could. We waited, holding our breath and listening hard, but no one came. So I flipped the light switch on.

"Let me see the camcorder, Lyndz." Straightaway Fliss rushed over and grabbed the camcorder.

"It's fine," said Lyndz. "Did you think I'd taken a bite out of it on the way downstairs, or something?"

"I just want to be sure," said Fliss. You can see why we call her Fusspot.

"Your mum's got loads of stuff, Fliss," said Rosie. She was standing behind the sofa, looking at a china lady in a green dress, which stood on a small table.

"Don't touch anything," Fliss said nervously. "My mum'll get in a real razz if anything gets broken. Some of these things cost a lot of money."

We all looked round the living room. I think I've told you about it before, haven't I?

It's like every other room in Fliss's house, all neat and clean and cream-coloured. And there are hundreds and hundreds of ornaments everywhere, things like china ladies wearing old-fashioned costumes, toby jugs and big glass bowls. There are so many things in it, you're almost frightened to move, in case you accidentally knock something over. Fliss is always going on about how much her mum's stuff cost, but some of it looked pretty nasty to me, although I was too polite to say so. That china lady in the green dress that Rosie was looking at, for instance, was gross.

"Let's get started," said Lyndz with an enormous yawn. "I'm going to fall asleep soon if we don't."

"Come on then, Kenny." I looked at her. "What's this super-cool plan of yours to get us on *You've Been Framed* then?"

Kenny grinned.

"A Human Pyramid," she said.

We all looked at each other.

"Excuse me?" I said. "I thought you said a Human Pyramid."

"I did."

"What, you mean when people stand on each other's shoulders?" Rosie asked.

"I've seen that on the telly," said Lyndz. "Only the people at the bottom were riding about on motorbikes, with the others standing on top of them."

Fliss was looking a bit sick. "Do you think that's going to work, Kenny?"

"Just a minute, give me a chance to explain," Kenny said confidently. "We won't be able to do it exactly right—"

"You're telling me," I remarked. "It's going to be a pretty sad human pyramid with only four of us."

"I know that," Kenny said. "I suppose I was thinking more of a Human Tower."

"A Human Tower?" Rosie repeated.

"Yep, one person's at the bottom, and then someone climbs up and sits on their shoulders, and then someone sits on *their* shoulders and so on." Kenny beamed at us. "What do you think?"

"It'll never work," said Lyndz.

"That's the point," Kenny said triumphantly. "We want it to go wrong, don't we? Then it'll be funny. Trust me."

When Kenny says "Trust me", it's like telling someone to trust Count Dracula when he's feeling a bit peckish. We all looked nervously at each other.

"Who's the unlucky idiot who's going to be at the bottom holding everyone else up?" I asked. Kenny grinned at me. "Oh no, you're joking."

"Well, you are the tallest, Frankie." Kenny said cheerfully. "And the strongest."

"Who'll be at the very top then?" asked Lyndz.

Kenny shrugged.

"It's got to be Fliss, who else?" She beamed at Fliss. "See, I told you you'd be the star."

Fliss looked a bit more cheerful. "Well, I suppose we could give it a go," she said.

Kenny looked thoughtfully up at the chandelier light fitting in the middle of the room.

"If we can get up high enough, Fliss could swing across the room like Tarzan on her mum's chandelier."

Now Fliss didn't look quite so keen.

"Kenny—" she began.

"Oh, come on, Kenny," I said. "Be serious."

Kenny grinned. "OK, I was only joking."

Fliss heaved a huge sigh of relief. "Are you ready with the camera, Lyndz?" she said.

Lyndz put the camera to her eye, and gave us a thumbs-up.

"Right, me first then," Kenny jumped up onto the arm of the sofa, and grabbed my shoulders. "Bend down a bit, Frankie, and let me climb onto you."

"Why do I always have to be the one who does all the hard bits?" I grumbled, but I crouched down and let Kenny get onto my shoulders, with her legs dangling in front. It was a bit difficult to stand up with Kenny's dead weight on top of me but I just about managed it.

"See?" Kenny waved at the others, and began bouncing up and down on my shoulders with excitement. "I told you it'd work – woh! Stand still, Frankie!"

I was trying to stand still, but my knees kept buckling under me, and I couldn't stop myself staggering from side to side.

"Ow!" I complained as Kenny grabbed at my hair. "I'm going to be bald soon at this rate!"

"Well, keep still, can't you?" Kenny hissed. "If you didn't keep moving around, I wouldn't have to hold on. Now bend down so Rosie can get onto my back."

I tried to bend down, but I couldn't. My knees kept on wobbling and I was scared I was going to fall over. I could hardly hold Kenny up, and Rosie and Fliss had to get on board yet.

Fliss had now gone right off the idea. She was dancing round us, looking more and more agitated. "Stop it!" she was wailing. "You're going to break something!"

Kenny ignored her.

"Come on, Rosie! Climb up onto my shoulders!"

My knees went before Rosie even made a move. I collapsed onto the sofa, throwing Kenny head first into a pile of cushions.

"Ouch!" Kenny complained, pulling herself upright. "What's the matter with you lot? That would have been excellent."

"Yeah, if I was Arnie Schwarzenegger," I said, rubbing my aching shoulders.

"You're crazy, Kenny," said Rosie. "It's too risky. We might break something."

"Yes," said Fliss, glaring at Kenny. "Now sit down where I can keep an eye on you."

We all sat down meekly on the cream-coloured sofa. Lyndz yawned, which started us all off.

"I'm so tired," Lyndz complained. "Let's forget it and go to bed."

"We can't forget about being on TV!" said Fliss. "This might be the only chance we ever get." She looked round at us, a little smile on her lips. "Actually, I've got an idea..."

"For *You've Been Framed*?" I said. That made us all sit up and stop yawning. "What is it?"

"It's really funny," said Fliss.

We all leant forward eagerly on the sofa.

"Tell us then," said Rosie.

"Well, first I'll have to go into the kitchen," said Fliss.

"Are we going to do some cooking like we did at the last sleepover here then?" asked Lyndz.

"You mean when Fliss's porridge went mad in the microwave?" I said.

"Oh, and remember Lyndz set off the smoke alarm when she was making toast," said Kenny.

"I nearly died laughing when Kenny's waffle mixture went walkies out of the waffle-maker," said Rosie. That started us all laughing, even Fliss.

"Now that would have been a brilliant video to send to *You've Been Framed*!" I said. "We'd have got on TV, no problem!"

"So are we going to do some more cooking then?" Lyndz asked eagerly.

"No." Fliss shook her head. "I'm just going into the kitchen to get some orange squash and biscuits."

"Great," said Kenny. "I'm starving."

"What about your *You've Been Framed* idea?" Lyndz asked.

"This *is* my idea," Fliss said impatiently. "I'll get the squash and biscuits, and hand them round. Then when I get to Kenny, I'll drop the plate and tip the biscuits all over her."

"And?" I said.

Fliss frowned. "There's no 'and'," she said. "That's it."

"That's IT?" I repeated. "That's IT?"

"It's not very funny, Fliss," Lyndz said. She was trying to be polite. What she really meant was that it wasn't funny at all.

"Of course it is," Fliss said confidently. "What do you think, Rosie?"

Rosie cleared her throat a couple of times. "Well – um – it might be funny, I suppose..." Her voice died away.

"I think it's a great idea," Kenny said unexpectedly. "I reckon we should give it a go."

My mouth fell open. I couldn't believe what I'd just heard. Fliss's idea was rubbish, so why wasn't Kenny saying so? What was she up to?

"Are you sure, Kenny?" Lyndz asked hesitantly.

Kenny nodded. "Yeah, I think it'll be excellent."

Fliss beamed at her. "Thanks, Kenny!" she said gratefully. "I'll go and get the squash and biscuits. Lyndz, get ready with the camera."

"We'll be ready," Kenny promised. "Oh, and Fliss, put some ice cubes in the orange squash, will you? I'm really hot and thirsty."

Fliss went off to the kitchen, smiling all over her face. Rosie went to help her, and Lyndz started fiddling with the camcorder, so that left me and Kenny on our own.

"What was all that about?" I asked.

"What do you mean?" Kenny said innocently.

"All that stuff with Fliss." I looked at Kenny closely. "You're up to something, Laura MacKenzie."

"Oh dear, what a suspicious mind you've got, Francesca Thomas." Kenny leaned back on the sofa, and put her hands behind her head. "As if I'd be up to anything."

I wasn't convinced. After all, I knew Kenny. But I couldn't see what on earth she was going to do. After all, there wasn't a lot that could go wrong with some orange squash and a plate of biscuits, was there? I mean, not even Kenny could manage to create a disaster out of that.

Could she?

CHAPTER EIGHT

Fliss and Rosie were in the kitchen for what seemed like ages, but eventually Rosie came out.

"Fliss says she's ready to bring the tray of squash and biscuits in," she announced. "She wants me, Frankie and Kenny sitting on the sofa, and Lyndz ready with the camera."

Lyndz gave Rosie a thumbs-up.

"I'm ready."

"So are we," Kenny said. "Did Fliss remember to put some ice cubes in the squash?"

Rosie nodded, and sat down next to me.

"What's with the ice cubes?" I said in

Kenny's ear. "That's the second time you've mentioned them."

Kenny shrugged.

"I'm just thirsty, that's all."

"We're not supposed to be stuffing our faces here, you know," I reminded her.

Kenny stuck her tongue out at me. "So what? I can still get a drink, can't I?"

I looked hard at her. There was something going on, but for the life of me I couldn't see what it was. I didn't have time to say anything else, because right at that moment Fliss popped her head round the kitchen door.

"I'm ready," she said, nodding at Lyndz. "Let's try and get it right first time, or we'll be running out of tape."

We all nodded solemnly. Personally, I couldn't see that it mattered whether we ran out of tape or not. Fliss spilling a plate of biscuits over Kenny was hardly going to provide laugh-a-minute stuff for a TV programme. But it was easier to sit there and do it than to argue with Fliss, so I stayed where I was between Rosie and Kenny.

Fliss came out of the kitchen with a silly

smile on her face. She was carrying a large blue tray which held four glasses, a plate of Hobnobs and a big jug of orange squash with ice cubes in it. It took her a while to get across to the sofa where we were sitting because she kept stopping to smile at the camera. But she made it eventually.

"Would everyone like some squash and biscuits?" she asked brightly, putting the tray down on the coffee table.

"Yes, please," we all chorused dutifully.

"I'll hand the biscuits round first," Fliss said meaningfully. She had her back to Lyndz, and she started winking at Kenny like mad. Kenny grinned at her, and nodded.

"Would you like a biscuit, Rosie?" Fliss asked, picking up the plate. I suppose she was going to ask me next, and then would come the Big Moment when she tipped the biscuits all over Kenny. Hilarious. But, of course, we didn't get that far. Rosie didn't even get a chance to reply to Fliss's question.

Because, as soon as Fliss turned to offer Rosie one of the Hobnobs, Kenny pounced. She leaned forward, scooped a couple of ice cubes out of the jug of squash and tipped them down the neck of Fliss's pyjama jacket.

From that moment on, everything moved so fast I'm still not sure what really happened. Of course, Fliss leapt a mile into the air when the ice cubes connected with her bare skin, although by some miracle she managed not to scream. When she leapt a mile, though, she still had the plate in her hand. Biscuits flew everywhere, as Fliss accidentally cracked the plate hard against Rosie's chin. Rosie gasped, and flung out her arms in shock. I was sitting next to her, and I didn't want to get hit in the eye, did I? So I leapt backwards onto the top of the sofa, out of harm's way.

Silly me. I leapt too hard. I teetered and wobbled on the top of the sofa for a few seconds, a bit like Lyndz had done on the bed earlier, and then I went over. My heels flew over my head, and I landed on the thick, fluffy carpet on the other side. Unfortunately I hit the little table on my way over, and I took the painted china lady in the nasty green dress with me. Well, most of her. Her head fell off when she hit the floor, and it rolled away under the dresser.

Feeling a bit dazed, I pulled myself upright. Four horrified faces were hanging over the sofa, looking down at me and at the headless body of the painted china lady lying next to me. In fact, Fliss's face was exactly the same nasty green colour as the lady's dress.

"Frankie, what have you done?" Rosie gasped.

"Me!" I said indignantly. "It wasn't my fault. Thanks a lot, Kenny."

"Sorry, Fliss," Kenny muttered. "I didn't know that was going to happen, did I?"

Fliss was almost crying.

"My mum's going to kill me. That ornament cost eighty pounds!"

"Calm down, Fliss," I said. "We might be able to fix it."

"Where's the head gone?" Lyndz asked.

"I think it rolled under the dresser," I said.

Kenny climbed off the sofa.

"I'll have a look." She lay down on the carpet, and pushed her arm under the dresser as far as it would go. "Got it!"

She pulled the lady's head out, and we all crowded round to look at it. Apart from the fact that it wasn't attached to her body anymore, there wasn't any other damage.

"Look, it'll be easy to repair it," Lyndz said, taking the head from Kenny and the body from me. "It broke off right around the neckline of the dress."

We all looked. Lyndz was right. It had been a clean break.

"We can fix it, Fliss," Lyndz said kindly, "And your mum will never even notice it's been broken, I swear."

"Really?" Fliss sniffed.

"No problem," said Lyndz. "But we need some glue."

Fliss frowned. "I'm not allowed to use the superglue," she said. "But I've got a Pritt stick in my school bag. Will that do?"

Lyndz nodded, and Fliss went out to fetch it.

"You seem to know a lot about mending things, Lyndz," Rosie said admiringly.

Lyndz shrugged. "When you've got four brothers, you get used to it," she said.

Fliss came back with the Pritt stick, and Lyndz carefully rubbed it over the top of the body and the bottom of the head. The rest of us picked up the broken biscuits, and then swept up the crumbs. Then we had to sit and wait for the pieces to stick. It took ages, even though we all took turns at pressing the two halves together. By this time it was 1.30 am, and we were all dead tired.

At last Lyndz said she thought the bits had stuck. We did a few tests like turning the lady upside down ten times in a row to see if the head fell off or not. It didn't.

Lyndz put the lady gently down on the coffee-table, and we all stood back and looked at it. It was amazing. You just couldn't tell that it had ever been broken. Well, only if you got down on your hands and knees and took a close look.

"Thanks, Lyndz," Fliss said gratefully. "You've saved my life."

"So can we please go to bed now?" Kenny said with an enormous yawn.

"We could have gone to bed ages ago if you hadn't been such an idiot," Fliss retorted with a sniff.

"OK, OK," said Kenny. "I said sorry, didn't I?"

"Sorry isn't enough," said Fliss. "You can be my slave for a week."

Kenny groaned. "Oh, all right then."

Fliss's eyes gleamed. I could tell that she was already starting to think up tasks for Kenny to perform.

"I *have* to go to bed NOW," said Rosie. "I'm falling asleep on my feet."

"I'm going to have some squash first." Kenny picked up the jug, and poured herself a glassful. "Oh, rats, all the ice cubes have melted."

"I should think you've had enough of ice cubes for a while," I remarked.

"I have," said Rosie. "And I never want to see *You've Been Framed* again, either."

"I never want to see a camcorder again," I said between yawns. "Ever."

"Where is the camcorder?" Fliss asked suddenly, looking wild-eyed with panic.

"It's OK, I turned it off when Frankie went over the sofa," Lyndz said. "I left it over there on the chair."

Lyndz went over to get it, but just as she bent over to pick the camcorder up, we all got a shock.

The living-room door was flung wide open.

CHAPTER NINE

Fliss's mum was standing in the doorway, blinking at us. We all nearly dropped down dead with shock.

"What on earth are you girls doing down here?" Mrs Sidebotham exclaimed. "It's a quarter to two!"

"Sorry, Mrs Sidebotham," we all mumbled. Out of the corner of my eye, I saw Lyndz sit down carefully in the armchair, so that the camcorder was hidden behind her. Meanwhile, Kenny had moved slightly closer to me, so that we were shoulder to shoulder and blocking Mrs Sidebotham's view of the china lady in the green dress who now had a broken neck.

"Well?" Mrs Sidebotham raised her eyebrows at us.

"We woke up and felt hungry," Fliss said quickly.

"And thirsty," Kenny chimed in.

"So we came downstairs for some squash and biscuits," Rosie finished off.

Mrs Sidebotham looked suspicious.

"You haven't been doing any cooking, have you?" she asked.

We all shook our heads virtuously.

"No, Mrs Sidebotham."

"Good." Fliss's mum looked mightily relieved. "Off to bed then, please. I don't know what your parents would think if they knew you were up at this time of night."

Yawning, we all stumbled over to the door. Except for Lyndz. She stayed where she was in the armchair.

"Come on, Lyndsey," said Fliss's mum impatiently. "Time for bed."

Lyndz stood up reluctantly. I guessed she was waiting for Mrs Sidebotham to go out of the room first, so she could grab the camcorder and bring it upstairs with her. But it was obvious that Fliss's mum wasn't going anywhere until she'd checked us all one by one.

As Lyndz came over to the door, we all looked anxiously at the chair where she'd been sitting. Fliss was standing next to me and I could feel her shaking in complete panic. But we needn't have worried. There was no sign of the camcorder anywhere. There was a big, fat, green cushion in the middle of the armchair, and somehow Lyndz must have managed to shove the camcorder behind it.

We all gave such a sigh of relief at exactly the same moment that I'm surprised Mrs Sidebotham didn't notice it. But then she wouldn't have. She was too busy staring at her painted china lady in the green dress.

"What have you girls been up to down here?" she asked suspiciously. "You've moved my Victorian lady."

We all froze to the spot. Fliss's knees were shaking so much, I swear it was only Rosie and me standing shoulder to shoulder on either side of her that held her up. The only one of us who had the nerve to say anything at all was Kenny.

"Oh, sorry, Mrs Sidebotham. That was my fault."

We all turned to stare at Kenny in amazement, and if looks could kill, Fliss would have murdered Kenny on the spot. But Kenny didn't take any notice.

"It's so pretty, I picked it up to have a closer look at it," she went on. "I hope you don't mind."

Fliss's mum looked pleased.

"Yes, it is pretty, isn't it? I don't mind you looking at my things, Laura, but do be careful, won't you?" She reached out, and turned the figure slightly to the left. Holding it by its head. We all watched in breathless terror. We expected the head to come off in her hands like something in a horror movie, but it didn't.

"Now – BED," said Fliss's mum firmly, and we all scrambled up the stairs as fast as we could. None of us could believe quite how lucky we'd been that evening, and the sooner we were all tucked up in bed, the better. Besides, we were all asleep on our feet.

Fliss's mum came with us, and watched us

crawl into our beds and sleeping bags. "Now I don't want to hear a sound until morning," she warned us. "Not a single sound."

I yawned hugely. I wasn't going to argue with that. I'd never felt so tired in my whole life. Mrs Sidebotham switched the light out, and went away.

Then Fliss said in a low voice, "Lyndz, what did you do with the camcorder?"

"I shoved it behind the cushion," Lyndz said sleepily. "I couldn't think what else to do."

"We can't leave it there," Kenny said. "It's still got our tape in it."

"I'll go down and get it in a few minutes," Fliss said, in between yawns. "When my mum's gone to sleep again."

There was silence for a little while. No one even suggested singing our sleepover song because we were just too worn out. I curled up snugly inside my sleeping bag, and closed my eyes. What a night.

I started to drift off into sleep. But then Kenny, who was lying on the floor next to me, began to giggle softly.

"Shut up, MacKenzie," I said drowsily.

"Sorry," Kenny muttered. "I was just remembering Fliss's face when I dropped those ice cubes down her neck."

I thought back to that moment, and a picture of Fliss's horrified face swam into my mind too. I began to laugh, and I had to turn over and bury my face in my pillow.

"What are you two sniggering at?" asked Lyndz, who was lying on the other side of me.

"Fliss's face when those ice cubes went down her neck!" I blurted out between giggles. Kenny was too paralysed with laughter to say anything herself. There was silence for a few seconds, and then Lyndz's sleeping bag began to shake too.

"Shut up, you lot!" Rosie whispered. "I'm trying to get to sleep here!"

"What about when Fliss cracked Rosie on the chin with the plate of biscuits?" Lyndz spluttered helplessly. That set the three of us off again, and this time Rosie couldn't help joining in. We were practically all weeping with laughter.

"Shut up," said Fliss from the other bed. "I don't think it was very funny at all. Any of it."

"What, not even when Frankie went over the back of the sofa?" Kenny said. "With her arms and legs, she looked like a daddy-long-legs having a fit."

This time we all laughed, even Fliss. We just couldn't help ourselves. We laughed for ages. And we still had smiles on our faces when we fell asleep.

So now you know just about everything. You also know why we don't want anyone to find out what really happened last night. You can keep a secret, can't you? Course you can! You'd better – or I'll set Kenny on you.

Only kidding. I know I can trust you.

Well, there isn't really that much left for me to tell you. We all overslept this morning, because of going to bed so late last night. Usually we like getting up early when we sleepover at Fliss's because her mum makes great breakfasts. They've got a juicer and the famous waffle-maker, so we always pig out. But not this morning.

Even Andy and Fliss's mum overslept. The only one who didn't was Fliss's little brother Callum, who didn't bother waking anyone else up. Typical. We were all still snoring away when Kenny's dad arrived at ten o'clock to collect her, so the first we knew about it was Callum banging on Fliss's bedroom door. I was getting a lift home with Kenny, so I had to get up too.

"You look like the walking dead," Kenny remarked as we shoved our stuff into our sleepover bags.

"Yeah, well, you'd win a Miss Baggy-Eyes contest, no problem," I said.

The others were still dead to the world. Rosie opened one eye and said goodbye to us, but Fliss and Lyndz were just lumps under the bedclothes. Yawning, Kenny and I staggered out onto the landing, just as Fliss's mum hurried out of her bedroom.

"I'm sorry, girls," she gasped. "We should have been up hours ago. I'll make you some breakfast."

"It's OK, Mrs Sidebotham," Kenny said politely. "My dad's here to collect us."

"Oh dear." Fliss's mum looked guilty. "What on earth is he going to think?"

Kenny shrugged. "Don't worry about it," she said. But when we got downstairs, where

Kenny's dad was waiting in the hall, Mrs Sidebotham spent about ten minutes apologising for oversleeping.

"—and the girls never even got to watch their sleepover video!" she finished up. "I was looking forward to seeing that myself."

Kenny and I glanced at each other. Whoops. I didn't think Mrs Sidebotham would be that keen on the video if she saw the uncensored version. Anyway, she wouldn't be seeing it at all because Fliss would have collected the camcorder from behind the cushion and replaced our tape with a blank one by now.

"Oh, well, never mind." Dr MacKenzie opened the front door. "They can watch it another time. Are you ready, girls?"

"Thanks for having us, Mrs Sidebotham," we said politely, then we legged it down the path, and jumped into the car. For once, I was going to be glad to get home.

"I feel like I could sleep for a week," Kenny muttered in my ear.

"Me too," I said. "I was so tired last night, I didn't even hear Fliss go downstairs to get the camcorder."

"Me neither," Kenny said.

We looked at each other.

"But she must have done," Kenny went on confidently. "She wouldn't have forgotten."

"No," I agreed.

When I got home, my mum took one look at me and started tutting.

"Late night, Frankie?"

"What makes you think that?" I said.

"You could carry home ten pounds of potatoes in those bags under your eyes." My mum looked at me critically. "How was your video?"

"All right." I managed to look her straight in the eye. "We didn't get a chance to watch it though, because we all overslept."

"What a shame," my mum said. "Oh, well, you'll be pleased to know that your dad's now thinking of buying a camcorder. I've tried to put him off, but you know what your dad's like. He gets an idea into his head, and then it sticks." She smiled at me. "A bit like someone else I know."

"Oh, Mum," I yawned. "Dad's crazy. Camcorders are so over-rated. They're not that cool, really."

My mum looked at me suspiciously.

"You've changed your tune. What happened at Fliss's last night?"

"Oh, nothing," I said cautiously. "But once you've seen one camcorder, you've seen them all."

So that was that. I think my mum was a bit suspicious about what had gone on at Fliss's sleepover, but when nothing happened (Fliss's mum didn't ring up to complain, like she usually did), she stopped worrying. Anyway, my mum and I ganged up on my dad and told him that instead of having a camcorder, we'd rather use all that money to go on holiday.

So everything turned out all right in the end, didn't it? There aren't many sleepovers when that happens. I'm well in with Mum because nothing disastrous happened at the sleepover (or so she thinks), and also because we've persuaded my dad not to buy a camcorder. And I'm going on holiday. Excellent!

Look, that's my house at the end of the street. Why don't you come home and watch *Mrs Doubtfire* with us? My dad's making the famous Thomas pizza, and we've got popcorn and lemonade too. And I know you won't say a word to my parents about what I just told you.

Wait a minute, though.

See that red car parked outside our house?

Do you know whose car that is?

I do.

It's Fliss's mum's car.

GOODBYE

Panic stations! What do you think Fliss's mum is doing at my house? Yes, she knows my mum, and yes, she does call round sometimes, but it's a bit of a coincidence that she's calling round the night after a sleepover. Especially a sleepover when something completely drastic happened…

Maybe I left something at Fliss's house after the sleepover, and her mum's come to return it? No, I know I didn't. I remember unpacking everything.

So what's Fliss's mum doing at my house? It must be something important if she's come round to see my parents in person, rather than just phoning up. Something important or something serious…

What did you say? No, that can't be right. Fliss couldn't be so stupid… I mean, she said she was going to wait a few minutes until her mum was asleep again, and then she was going to go downstairs and get the camcorder back. I'm sure she wouldn't have forgotten. And if she'd got the camcorder, she definitely wouldn't have forgotten to take our tape out and put a new blank tape in. Fliss is too scared of getting into trouble with her mum to have forgotten to make sure we were in the clear.

But then again, we were all really tired, including Fliss… Maybe she was planning to go downstairs, and she just fell asleep without meaning to? Kenny and I should have checked this morning when we were getting ready to leave, but we were in a hurry to go home and Fliss didn't even wake up. Oh no. Do you think that the camcorder was still hidden behind the cushion this morning?

No, I don't believe it. Fliss must have gone downstairs after the rest of us were asleep. We just didn't hear her, that's all. Come on, we don't have to be nervous. Let's just go home calmly and sensibly, and find out exactly what Fliss's mum is doing here.

Quick, get behind that tree! Mrs Sidebotham's coming out of our house right now!

Did she see us? No, she's going over to her car. Can you see her face? What does she look like? Normal? Happy? Sad? Or just plain, downright FURIOUS? There's only one way to find out. I'll have to go home.

But you'll come with me, won't you? It's probably better if you don't come in at first, just in case mum and dad are waiting to tear me to bits. But I'm sure they won't be. I hope.

Here we are then. Why don't you go and wait by the living-room window, then you can see what's going on? If everything's OK, I'll give you a thumbs-up. Wish me luck!

The door opens. It's my mum.

"Oh, it's you, Frankie. You were a long time."

I look at my mum closely. She seems OK. She's not red in the face, and she's not glaring at me. That's a good sign.

"Sorry," I say. "It took me a really long time

to choose a video."

"What did you get?" my mum asks.

"*Mrs Doubtfire*." I hold the video out to show her. "I know we've seen it before, but you liked it so much, I thought I'd get it out again." Crawl, crawl.

"Good idea." My mum opens the door wider, and I go inside. But hang on a minute, we're not in the clear yet.

As soon as I see my dad pacing up and down the living room, I know that something's not quite right. My dad's not as good as my mum at keeping a straight face. I think you'd better stay outside the window for the moment. I've got a feeling things could start getting nasty in here.

"What video did you get, Frankie?" my dad asks in a voice that tells me something not very nice is about to happen.

"*Mrs Doubtfire*," I say cautiously. No use going looking for trouble, as my grandma always says, let it come and look for you. And, boy, was it coming to look for me right now.

"Oh, *Mrs Doubtfire*'s a brilliant film," my mum says. "But we've got an even better video than *Mrs Doubtfire* to show you."

"Oh?" I say, with a sinking heart. Now I know exactly why Fliss's mum had come round to our house.

"Sit down." says my dad.

"Well, actually, I don't feel much like watching a video right now," I start babbling nervously. "I think I'll go up to my room—"

"Sit down, Frankie," my mum says grimly.

I sit.

My dad picks up the remote control, and turns the TV on. A very familiar scene fills the TV screen. That's Kenny, Rosie and me, sitting in a row on Mrs Sidebotham's cream-coloured sofa. Then the camera swings round a little jerkily to show Fliss coming out of the kitchen, beaming all over her face and carrying a tray of orange squash and biscuits. We all watch in silence as Fliss puts the tray down on the coffee table, and then picks up the plate of biscuits. She turns to offer the biscuits to Rosie, and there, just at the very side of the picture, we can see Kenny's fingers dip into the jug of orange squash, and pull out some ice cubes. Then we see Kenny jump up and tip the ice down

Fliss's pyjama jacket.

I have to say that Lyndz would make a great film director when she grows up. She had managed to catch Fliss's horrified face perfectly, right in the middle of the screen, followed by the plate cracking against Rosie's chin. Then the camera had followed me quickly as I jumped up onto the back of the sofa, and it had captured my fall to the carpet in every detail. There is just one more shot of me in a heap on the floor with the headless figure of the china lady next to me, and then the picture goes black. That must have been when Lyndz switched the camera off.

No one says anything. Even though I know I'm now in deep doom forever, I just want to laugh my head off. I've never seen anything as funny as that video, not even on *You've Been Framed*. It's a classic. But I dare not even smile. If I do, I know I'll be in even bigger trouble.

When it's finally over, my dad turns off the TV.

"I think you'd better go to your room," says my mum. "We'll talk about this later when you've had time to think over what you've done."

Oh no, I hate it when they do that. Why can't they just give me my punishment now? At least then I know what I'm letting myself in for. But I'd better not argue.

I go quietly out of the room. Look, I think you'd better go. I'm going to be grounded for at least a year, so there's no point in you hanging around any more. Still, it was almost worth being grounded just to see that video. It's a shame we'll never get to send it to *You've Been Framed* now. I bet we would have got on TV, no problem.

As I'm going upstairs, I hear funny noises coming from the living-room. So I tiptoe back down, to find out what's going on. I put my ear to the door, and listen.

Guess what?

My mum and dad are laughing their heads off!

"Frankie and the others are going to have to pay for that figure they broke," my mum is saying.

My dad is too busy laughing to reply for a few seconds.

"Come on, let's watch it again. I've never seen anything as hilarious in my whole life!"

I hear the sound of the video being rewound, and then the sound of my mum and dad laughing again.

"That's just a classic," says my dad. "You know what? It's a shame we can't send this to *You've Been Framed*. I'm sure they'd show it."

I couldn't believe what I was hearing. Parents! Aren't they enough to make you sick?

But maybe that means I'll get off without being grounded for the rest of my life.

Wish me luck.

See ya!

The Sleepover Club at Frankie's

Join the Sleepover Club: Frankie, Kenny, Felicity, Rosie and Lyndsey, five girls who just want to have fun – but who always end up in mischief.

Brown Owl's in a bad mood and the Sleepover Club are determined to cheer her up. Maybe she'd be happier if she had a new boyfriend. And where better than a sleepover at Frankie's to plan Operation Blind Date?

Pack up your sleepover kit and drop in on the fun!

0 00 675233 0
£2. 99